FORTUNATELY

Written and illustrated by
REMY CHARLIP

Parents' Magazine Press
A Division of Parents' Magazine Enterprises, Inc.
New York

THIS BOOK IS DEDICATED TO NED AND CLAUDE AND THE PAPER BAG PLAYERS

Fortunately
one day, Ned got a letter that said,
"Please Come to a Surprise Party."

*But unfortunately
the party was in Florida
and he was in New York.*

*Fortunately
a friend loaned him an airplane.*

*Unfortunately
the motor exploded.*

Fortunately
there was a parachute in the airplane.

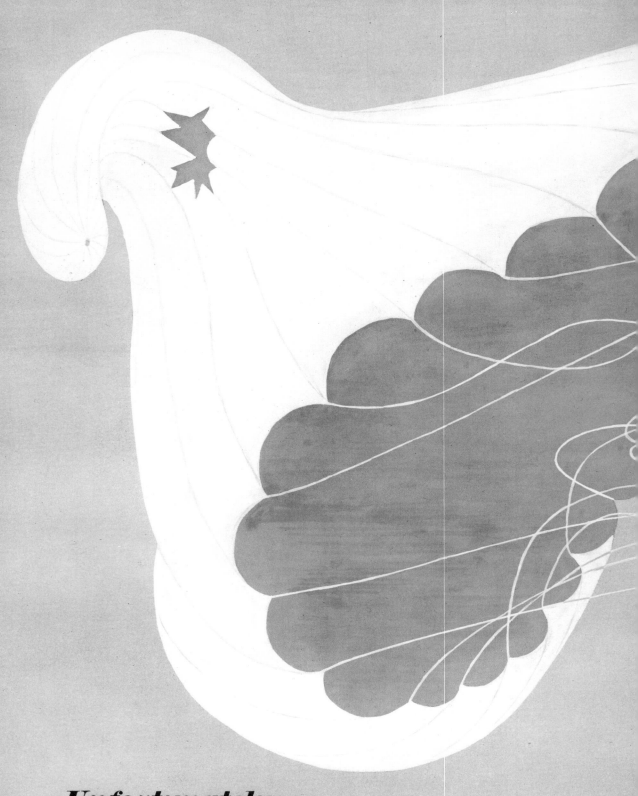

**Unfortunately
there was a hole in the parachute.**

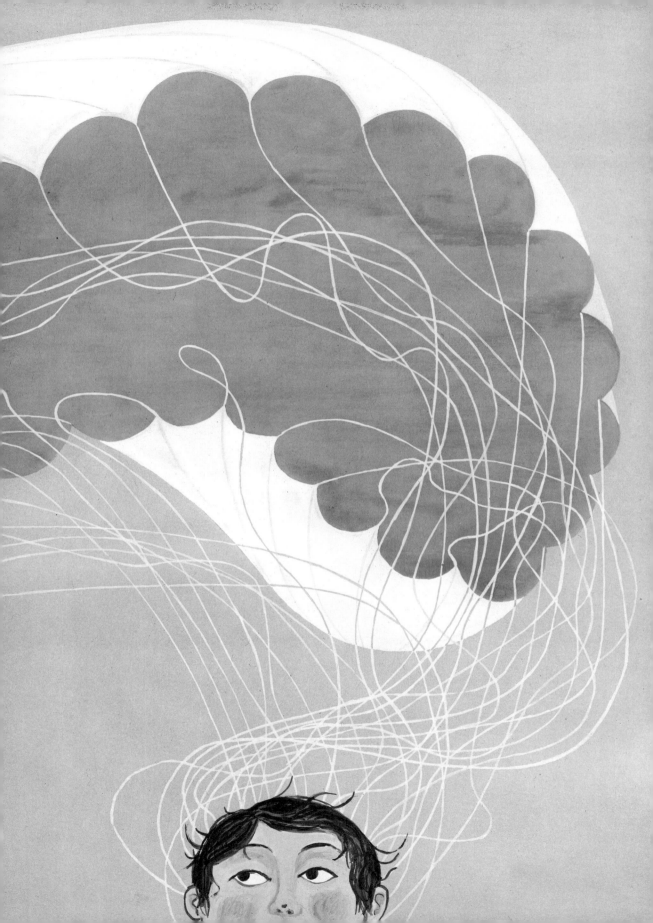

Fortunately
there was a haystack on the ground.

**Unfortunately
there was a pitchfork in the haystack.**

Fortunately
he missed the pitchfork.

**Unfortunately
he missed the haystack.**

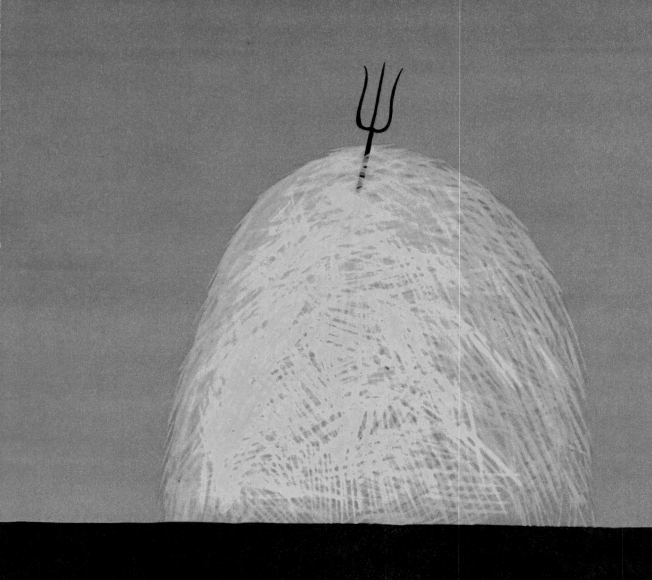

**Fortunately
he landed in water.**

Unfortunately there were sharks in the water.

Fortunately
he could swim.

*Unfortunately
there were tigers on the land.*

Fortunately
he could run.

Unfortunately
he ran into a deep dark cave.

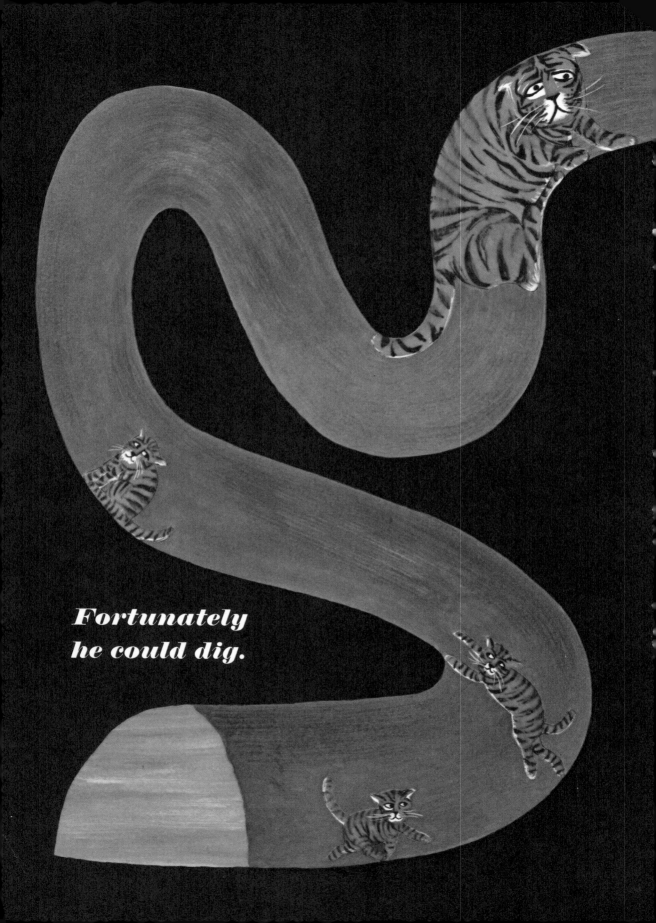

**Fortunately
he could dig.**

Unfortunately he dug himself into a fancy ballroom.

**Fortunately
there was a surprise party going on.
And fortunately
the party was for him,
because fortunately
it was his birthday!**